Crazy
Charlie

For Hogan and James

Published by Hinkler Books Pty Ltd
45–55 Fairchild Street
Heatherton Victoria 3202 Australia
www.hinkler.com.au

hinkler

First published by Andersen Press Ltd., London

Text © Ruth Brown 1979
Illustrations © Ruth Brown 1979
Cover design © Hinkler Books 2011

Cover design: Peter Tovey
Prepress: Graphic Print Group

ISBN: 978 1 7418 4204 3

Printed and bound in China

Crazy Charlie

Ruth Brown

hinkler

In the jungle, by the river, lived the biggest crocodile in the whole world. Crazy Charlie. That is what the other animals called him. He had the most enormous teeth and he ate everything he saw.

He started off in a small way, just munching
the odd floating log or canoe. But then he
got more ambitious and started to eat jetties
and motor boats and bicycles.
In fact anything or anyone anywhere near
the river at any time was in danger of being
crunched up by Charlie's mighty teeth.

People all over the world were shocked and horrified, but this only made Crazy Charlie worse, because the more famous he became the more he showed off.

He started eating houses and trains and factories. Things had gone too far!

The people called in the Army. The soldiers showered Charlie with arrows, to frighten him away, but he caught them and used them as toothpicks.

They shot at him with cannon but Charlie
caught the cannonballs and crunched them
up like gobstoppers.

They even fired a guided missile at him, but he ate that too–and enjoyed it. The people were in despair. But Crazy Charlie was having the time of his life being the centre of the world's attention.

But one day something terrible happened to Charlie. One by one his huge, beautiful, sharp teeth began to fall out.

Finally he was totally toothless. The crowds didn't come any more; nobody was frightened of him; nobody made a fuss. He was no longer big news. Life was very dull for Crazy Charlie. But the other animals enjoyed the peace and quiet.

One day Charlie saw a tourist, the first he'd seen for about six months. The man, who was collecting plants, looked absolutely terrified when he stumbled over the crocodile dozing by the river.

But Charlie knew that there was no point in trying to frighten the man. Who's afraid of a gummy crocodile anyway? So he just gave him a toothless grin instead.

The man was so relieved that he smiled at Charlie.
"I know just what you need," he said. "I'll send you some when I get home."

Charlie thought no more about him until a few months later when a large parcel arrived for him. It was from the plant-collecting tourist. He was a dentist and he had made Charlie the most beautiful set of sparkling teeth!

Charlie
Crocodile.
The Jungle

Crazy Charlie put them in his mouth and smiled the shiniest smile anyone had ever seen. People started flocking to see him once more, and how Charlie loved it! He was big news again, the centre of the world's attention, but now all he had to do was SMILE.